LEGENDS

BEASTS AND MONSTERS

LEGENDS

ANTHONY HOROWITZ

BEASTS AND MONSTERS

Illustrated by Thomas Yeates

MACMILLAN CHILDREN'S BOOKS

First published 2010 by Macmillan Children's Books

This edition published 2013 by Macmillan Children's Books
a division of Macmillan Publishers Limited
20 New Wharf Road, London N1 9RR
Basingstoke and Oxford
Associated companies throughout the world
www.panmacmillan.com

ISBN 978-1-4472-5470-6

1 3 5 7 9 8 6 4 2

A CIP catalogue record for this book is available from
the British Library.

Printed and bound by CPI Group (UK) Ltd, Croydon, CR0 4YY

CONTENTS

INTRODUCTION

This is not a new book. In fact, I wrote most of these myths and legends a very long time ago. I was twenty-eight at the time and in bed with glandular fever. Over a period of three months, I wrote (or rather, retold) thirty-five stories, and these were published in a book called THE KINGFISHER BOOK OF MYTHS AND LEGENDS. It's rather frightening to think that they have been in print now for almost thirty years.

The good news is that they're back in a completely new shape. The stories have been reinvented, with brand new illustrations, and they're published in six smaller editions.

A quick note on the thinking behind these re-tellings.

I've always loved myths and legends but some of the versions that I read when I was in my teens tended to be a bit dry. That is to say, they didn't have many jokes. There wasn't enough blood. The authors always made me feel that I was reading something serious and important just because the stories were so famous and so ancient – and the language they used was almost deliberately old-fashioned. It was a bit like walking around a museum, looking at dusty relics behind glass cases with 'Do Not Touch' signs all over the place.

Lying in bed with my grapes and *Beano* comics, I made two decisions. First of all, I would have fun. I would try to write the stories as if they were being told for the first time. Just because I was dealing with heroes and gods, I wouldn't be too reverential. And I also wanted to cast my net wide. I wouldn't just tell the stories that everyone knew – the Trojan Horse, the Minotaur, and so on. Nearly all the most famous stories come from the Ancient Greeks. But every culture has its own myths and legends. So I would also look at the tales of the Chinese, the Egyptians, the Cheyenne Indians, the Celts, the Incas and so on, all around the world.

Anyway, this is the result of my work all those years ago. I must confess that I have taken this opportunity to rewrite some of the stories a bit. Reading them again, I took out some of the more feeble jokes. I shortened some of the descriptions and cut bits that I thought were boring. And just for the hell of it, I've added a couple of new myths and legends. In this book, for example, you'll find the story of THE WASHER AT THE FORD, which I've always wanted to tell.

It's amazing to think how much has happened since I started work on this collection. When I first wrote these stories (on a typewriter – there were no computers then), I wasn't married. My two sons hadn't been born. I was renting a room in a flat in West London. And a certain Alex Rider didn't exist, not even as a flicker in my mind.

It was all a long time ago. But the stories existed a very long time before that. In fact they've existed for centuries and provided we keep on telling them, they will surely survive for centuries more.

Anthony Horowitz

THE RIDDLE OF THE SPHINX

Greek

'What creature has four legs in the morning, two legs in the afternoon and three legs in the evening?'

This was almost certainly the first riddle ever invented. It was told by a ghastly creature that had arrived one day outside the city of Thebes in Ancient Greece. The creature was called the Sphinx and it had the head of a woman, the body of a lion, the wings of an eagle and the tail of a snake. There was only one road to Thebes and you could not get into the city without passing the creature. And you could not pass the creature (which was also very large and very fast) without being asked the riddle.

One of the first people who came across the Sphinx was a young man called Haemon. He had been on his way to see his uncle, who happened to be the King of Thebes, when he found his way blocked. Many other people would have run away from so bizarre a mixture of bird, beast, snake and woman, but Haemon, coming from royal stock, was afraid of nothing.

'Stand where you are!' the Sphinx demanded with the voice of an angry schoolteacher. Its tail writhed in the dust and its wings beat at the air.

'What do you want?' Haemon asked, his hand falling to his sword.

'I have a riddle for you,' the Sphinx said.

'A riddle?' Haemon relaxed. 'That sounds fun. What is it?'

'What creature has four legs in the morning, two legs in the afternoon and three legs in the evening?'

'Well . . . let me see now. Four legs in the morning? It's not a dog or anything like that? I did once see a goat with three legs, but it wasn't alive so I suppose that doesn't count. A frog perhaps? I don't know. I give in . . .'

The words were no sooner out of his mouth than the Sphinx pounced. Using its wings, it leaped up in the air. Then its tail slithered round Haemon's neck and began to tighten. And finally, while its woman's

face laughed insanely, its claws tore him into several pieces and in seconds the road was slippery with blood – which is one of the very earliest jokes, for 'haimon' is the Greek word for 'bloody'. But Haemon, who was by this time being devoured, did not find it very funny.

Nor did the people of Thebes. When they discovered that it was impossible to get anywhere near the city without being confronted by a horrible monster, asked an impossible riddle, and torn apart when you failed to get it right, they almost had a riot. But there was nothing they could do. It was a bad year for business in Thebes. The bottom fell out of the tourism industry. Although King Laius and Queen Jocasta – who ruled over the city – offered a huge reward to anyone who could rid them of the Sphinx, the prize was never claimed.

Of course, princes and warriors came from far and wide to chance their arm against the creature, but it could not be destroyed by sword or arrow. Its hide was as hard as iron. Its huge claws were razor-sharp. Its wings would carry it into the air and its tail would tighten round your throat before you could blink. Some people tried to answer the riddle. As the months passed, all manner of answers were tried: rats, bats, cats, gnats and ocelots were just some of the unsuccessful ones. Every day another scream would split the air and fresh blood would splatter on the road.

Eventually the situation became so bad that the king decided he would have to do something about it himself.

'If only we knew why this horrible creature was here,' he said, 'we might be able to find a way to get rid of it.'

'Why not ask the Oracle?' Queen Jocasta suggested.

The Oracle was the name given to a priestess who could not only tell the future but also answer any question put to her. As soon as the queen had mentioned it, Laius wondered why he had never thought of the Oracle himself.

'An excellent idea, my dear,' he said. 'I'll set off at once.'

Now, had King Laius ever reached the Oracle, he would have had a nasty shock. For the truth of the matter was that it was entirely his own fault that the Sphinx was there – even if he didn't know it.

A short while before, Laius had gone to stay with a friend of his and had taken a fancy to the friend's son. In fact, he had gone so far as to carry off the boy, Chrysippus, and keep him locked up as a servant in his palace at Thebes. Eventually Chrysippus had killed himself, and that might have been that, had not the entire episode been witnessed by Hera, the queen of the gods. It was to punish King Laius that she had sent the Sphinx to Thebes.

But King Laius never reached the Oracle and never found this out. For, driving along the road in his chariot, he came across a

young man who was actually on his way to Thebes to challenge the Sphinx. It was a narrow road and there wasn't enough room for the two of them to pass. They exchanged angry words. Then King Laius drove his chariot over the young man's foot. The young man, who had a rather violent temper, responded by hurling his spear through the king's stomach before continuing on his way.

The young man was called Oedipus. He was quite a complex character. He was not really a bad man, despite his temper. He genuinely wanted to be a hero but didn't know how to go about it. Anyway, he now turned up outside the city of Thebes and confronted the Sphinx.

'Stand where you are!' the Sphinx cried. 'And tell me – if you value your life – what creature has four legs in the morning, two legs in the afternoon and three legs in the evening?'

Oedipus thought about it while the Sphinx

licked its lips and practised curling and un-
curling its claws. But this time it was not to
be so lucky.

'I have it,' Oedipus said at last. 'The answer is man. For in the morning, when he is
a baby, he crawls on all fours. In the afternoon of his life, he walks upright on two
legs. And when he is old, in the evening, he
walks with the aid of a stick.'

When the Sphinx heard that its riddle had
at last been guessed, it went red with anger.
Its woman's head screamed, its lion's body
writhed, the feathers fell out of its eagle's
wings and its serpent's tail shrivelled up.
Then it leaped into the air and exploded,
and that was the end of it.

As for Oedipus, he was given the crown
of Thebes as his reward and married Queen
Jocasta. He never suspected for a single
minute that she was in actual fact his long-
lost mother and that it was his father whom
he had killed on the road . . .

But that is very definitely another story.

THE INCREDIBLE SPOTTED EGG

Cheyenne Indian

The Incredible Spotted Egg

The Cheyenne Indians, who rode the plains of North America in the seventeenth and eighteenth centuries, had a strange custom. Whenever they came to a wide stretch of water – a lake or a river, perhaps – they would throw some food or tobacco in before they rode across. Nobody asked the Cheyennes why they did this, but then, of course, nobody asked the Cheyennes anything. If you met a Cheyenne in eighteenth-century America, it was safer just to run away.

But there was a reason. It was to be found in a tale told by the Cheyenne storytellers, a tale about a great river monster and two brothers who discovered an incredible spotted egg.

The two brothers were known simply as Elder and Younger and they had managed to get themselves lost on the prairie. The sun was beating down and the horizon formed a great big circle all around them with nothing – not a tree, not a building – to interrupt the unbroken line. They were surrounded by wild grass waving in the wind, and here and there they stumbled across the bleached-out bones of animals that had had the misfortune to wander into this desolate place. The brothers had a little water, but they had no food. They could feel their strength beginning to run out.

They walked a few miles and they got hungrier and hungrier, and soon the rumble of their stomachs was as loud as the rustle of the wind. Then all of a sudden, and completely unexpectedly, they came upon an egg, just lying on the ground with no sign of a bird or a nest anywhere near.

'The Great Spirit has been good to us,' Younger said. 'Look at that egg. I reckon it will last the two of us a whole week.'

'I'm not so sure,' Elder growled. 'It doesn't look good to me.'

'What do you mean?' Younger cried. 'It's just an egg.'

But if it was just an egg, it was certainly a very peculiar one. For a start, it was bright green with red spots. Also it was enormous – much bigger than a chicken's egg. Much bigger, in fact, than a chicken. And how had it got there? It was, after all, in the middle of nowhere.

'It looks bad magic to me,' Elder said. 'I say we don't touch it.'

'Where is your courage?' Younger replied. 'This egg was laid by a great bird, or perhaps a turtle. You are right, my brother. It is

a strange, a funny colour. But my stomach is empty. If I do not eat soon, I will be joining my ancestors. I would eat this egg if it was the colour of a tiger beetle. In fact, I would eat a tiger beetle too, cooked on a fire with cactus juice . . .'

So while Elder watched, Younger lit a bonfire and roasted the egg. Then he cracked the shell and began to eat.

'Are you sure you do not want to eat some of this, my brother?' he asked.

'No, thank you,' Elder said.

'It is powerful good. You cannot imagine what you're missing.'

In fact, Younger was lying when he said that. The egg was hard and rubbery. The yolk was green, the same colour as the shell, and the white wasn't white but a sort of pink. And it didn't taste like an egg should. It tasted of fish.

Even as Younger ate he began to feel sick, but something made him go on eating. He couldn't stop. Faster and faster he spooned the egg down until it had all gone and only the shell was left.

'I hope you know what you're doing,' Elder muttered.

The next morning, when they woke up, Younger was feeling really ill. His stomach was like a funfair merry-go-round and his eyes were as big as ping-pong balls. Worst of all, he was really thirsty. He drank all the water in his bottle, but it could have been a thimbleful for all the good it did him. Elder looked at him and sighed.

'You look terrible,' he said.

'I feel terrible,' Younger agreed.

'You're green!'

'Green?'

'And you've got red spots.'

Younger stood up. 'Let's go!' he said. 'The sooner we find water, the better. I need a drink.'

They walked until sunset, by which time Younger's skin had turned a brilliant shade of green and his red spots had got larger

and more distinctive too. All his hair had fallen out and he seemed to be having trouble talking.

'Ssssso,' he hissed. 'Do you think I made a missssstake eating that egg?'

'I think so, my brother,' Elder replied.

'I supposssse it was ssssstupid. But I will feel better when I get to water. I really want a ssssswim.'

The next morning Younger was worse. His arms had somehow glued themselves to his sides and his nose had dropped off. He was a vivid green and red and his skin was slimy. Like a toad's.

'I feel worssssse,' he moaned.

'You look worse,' Elder said.

'Water!'

They reached water at sunset. It was a river, frothing and bubbling, twisting through the hostile landscape. Shrubs and flowers were sprouting close to its banks. There would have to be a settlement close by. Their people would choose to live close to a river like this.

Younger, whose legs had almost melted into one another, decided that he would rather sleep in the river while Elder curled up on land beside a bonfire. Elder hadn't eaten for five days now and he was weak and tired.

It didn't take him long to fall asleep.

He was woken up by the sound of a strange, unearthly singing. He opened his eyes, and the first thing he saw was a great heap of fish lying on the bank, waiting to be cooked. Then he looked beyond, in the water, and saw his brother.

Except that it wasn't really his brother any more. Younger had become an enormous sea-monster with pointed teeth, bright silver scales and a forked tail. He was swimming to and fro, stopping now and then to fork another fish with the point of his tail and flip it on to the bank.

'Good morning, my brother!' Elder called out. 'How are you feeling today?'

'Sssstrong!' Younger replied. 'It'sssss not sssssso bad being a sssssea-ssssserpent. And I've caught a whole lot of fissssssh!'

'You have my thanks!' Elder said.

'Then – lisssssten,' Younger continued. 'Don't you forget about me. I got you food, sssssso you get me food. I don't want to eat

fisssssh all my life.'

'I'll do that,' Elder promised.

'And tobacco too. Just because I'm a monssssster, it don't mean I can't ssssssmoke!'

And that is why the Cheyennes always stopped and threw food or tobacco into the water before they crossed it (even when they were being chased by the cavalry). It was to keep the sea-serpent singing.

THE DRAGON AND SAINT GEORGE

English

There are no dragons today – mainly thanks to the knights and heroes who so thoughtlessly rode about the place killing them off. This is a pity, for dragons must have been astonishing creatures: part snake and part crocodile, with bits of lion, eagle and hawk thrown in for good measure. Not only could they leap into the air and fly (a tremendous feat when you think how heavy their scales must have been) but they could also run at great speed. Not that a dragon would ever run away. Dragons were generally very brave creatures. When they were angry or frightened, smoke would come hissing out of their nostrils. When things got really rough, flames would rush out of their mouths. But there was no such thing as a cowardly dragon.

Only the Chinese understood and admired the dragon. It was often said that some of the greatest Chinese emperors had been born the sons of dragons. Dragon bones and teeth were used as medicine. A dragon guarded the houses of the Chinese gods and brought rain to the earth when the crops needed it. That is why the Chinese still fly dragon kites and honour the dragon by including paper models of it in their New Year celebrations. The Chinese really did like the dragon.

But in fourth-century Palestine – when Saint George was alive – dragons were more feared than admired. It is true that they did have some unsettling habits. They tended to live in rather dank and nasty caves, for example, often guarding huge piles of treasure which had almost certainly been stolen from somebody else. They also had an unhealthy appetite for human flesh, their favourite food being princesses – although any young woman would do. But they were not the only man-eating animal on the globe. It was just that they got all the bad publicity.

Anyway, Saint George was the most famous dragon-killer of all – which is strange because he never actually killed a dragon.

The other strange thing is that, although he is best known today as the patron saint of England, George (as he was known before he became a saint) wasn't even English. He was actually born in Palestine.

His father was a high-ranking officer in the Roman army and for a time George followed in his footsteps, serving as a soldier under the Emperor Diocletian. He was brought up by Christian parents and he travelled the world, spreading the gospel and doing good.

His encounter with the dragon happened at a small town called Silene. And this is where the story begins.

The people of Silene had lived in fear of the dragon for many years. It lived in a cave on the edge of a stagnant lagoon, a few miles from the town. Now the vapours from this lagoon would often be carried by the wind into the town and the people came to believe that the dragon was responsible for the rotten smell that seeped through their streets. So they began to feed the dragon two sheep every day in the hope that it would go away. This was, of course, a particularly stupid idea and had exactly the opposite effect. Because once the dragon got used to the idea that it was going to receive a free meal at twelve o'clock regularly, it decided that the townspeople must be genuinely fond of it and actually wanted it to stay. Certainly it had no idea that they were afraid.

This went on for a number of years until, not surprisingly, the townspeople began to run out of sheep. So a council was called at which all the local politicians, along with the king himself, met to decide what to do.

The minister for external affairs was the first to speak. 'My honourable friends,' he began. 'This is a serious situation. Indeed, I am tempted to say that this is a crisis. We have no chops. We have no shepherd's pie. We have a shortage of wool. And why? Because we have given away all our sheep! And still this dragon refuses to go away.'

'Hear! hear!' all the other councillors cried, although in fact the minister hadn't said anything that they didn't already know.

The leader of the opposition got to his feet. 'I would like to remind the council,' he said, 'that I was always opposed to the policy of giving sheep to the dragon. If we had given it chickens, as I suggested, we would not now be facing this crisis. This is another example of government incompetence.

The government's behaviour can only be described as . . . sheepish!'

His friends all laughed at this rather feeble joke. But now the minister for internal affairs leaped up. 'The council's policy of giving sheep to the dragon has been a great success,' he said. 'Even though it is true that the dragon has not gone away yet, all the signs are that it will go away quite soon. We just need to feed it a bit more.'

There was a general outbreak of booing and shouting. Papers were waved, torn up and scattered until the Speaker, who was in charge of the council, had to call for order.

The minister for ministerial affairs stepped forward. 'If, as my honourable friend suggests, we are running out of sheep,' he suggested, 'we could try giving it something else.'

This produced a sudden hush as the other councillors considered the alternatives.

Then the king spoke, and his face was grim. 'It is well known,' he said, 'that dragons like the taste of children. It seems to me, therefore, that there is no alternative. We must give him our children. Once a week we will feed the dragon with our sons and daughters.'

For a moment, nobody spoke. The entire council was alarmed, but nobody wanted to argue with the king. After all, they had their careers to think about.

'I'm not sure this will go down well with the voters,' someone muttered.

'How will we choose the children?' someone else asked.

'We will have a lottery,' the king replied. 'Every child in the town will be given a number. Once a week a number will be drawn out of a hat. The child that has that number will be given to the dragon in order to save the town.' He rose to his feet. 'That is my law,' he concluded. 'There are to be no exceptions.'

Three months passed, during which time no fewer than a dozen children were seized by the royal guard, torn away from their weeping parents and then tied up and left outside the dragon's cave. Seven boys and five girls met this terrible end, the flesh picked so cleanly from their bones that the little skeletons gleamed pure white in the morning sunlight. As for the dragon, it noticed the change in its feeding. It was even a trifle puzzled. But the king had been quite right to say that it would like the taste. In fact it had been getting bored with sheep and found the children a welcome change. Needless to say, if it had been thinking about

moving on, it now decided to stay exactly where it was and even considered inviting a few friends to join it.

By the time George arrived, an atmosphere had descended on Silene more poisonous than any mist that had been blown in from

the lagoon. Every Tuesday, the day of the lottery, the streets were so silent that if the town had become a cemetery nobody would have noticed the difference. Few people left their homes, and those that did went about their business with pale faces, their mouths stretched in a grimace of fear, each avoiding the others' eyes. Then at midday a bell would ring. Soldiers would knock on the door of a house somewhere in the town. A terrible cry of pain and depair would break the silence. And everywhere parents would hug their children and thank the gods that their number had not been drawn.

George came on a Tuesday afternoon, a few hours after one of the lotteries had ended. It didn't take him long to find out what was happening in Silene and when he did find out he shook his head, half in astonishment, half in despair. Straight away he went to the palace to find the king, and as he walked into the throne room he heard the following conversation.

'You can't!' the king was saying. 'I forbid it!'

'But you told us to,' one minister replied.

'You made the law,' a second said.

'And you said no exceptions,' a third added.

'But she is a princess . . . my daughter.' Tears ran down the king's cheeks. 'She didn't even tell me that she had been given a number. When I find the idiot who gave her a number, I'll have him executed. I'll have him flayed alive!'

'It was the minister of the interior,' the minister of the exterior exclaimed.

'No it wasn't, Your Majesty!' the minister of the interior cried. 'As a matter of fact, I was the one who said that the royal family and all politicians should be exempt, that none of us should have to draw numbers. But she took one anyway. She said she wanted to be like all the other children.'

This was in fact true. The princess, although she was only fourteen years old, had been horrified by the turn of events in Silene. She was an intelligent and educated girl and, some might say, well ahead of her time. For example, she had argued passionately that criminals shouldn't be put to death before they'd even been tried and that perhaps it was a bad idea to wage war at the drop of a hat without thinking about the consequences. And she had been one of the first to speak out against this evil lottery. When the king had refused to listen to her, she had decided to take a stand. She had insisted on being given a number herself and, when it had been drawn, she had presented herself to the soldiers without any argument. Perhaps, when she was killed, her father would change his mind about this foolish law. That, at least, was what she hoped.

The king had changed his mind. But it seemed it was too late.

'She's already gone to the cave,' the minister for the interior explained. 'In fact, I'm

afraid she'll already have been devoured.'

'My only child!' the king wept. And for the first time he understood some of the suffering of his people. 'My princess . . . !'

George realized that there was no time to waste. He left the palace without even introducing himself, leaped on to his horse and rode out of the town in the direction of the lagoon. It wasn't difficult to find. The stench from the stagnant water was so strong that he could literally follow his nose.

The sound of weeping told him that he had found the cave and that, contrary to what the minister had said, he was not too late. The dragon had overslept that day and the princess was still alive, sitting on the ground with her hands tied behind her back. George got off his horse and walked over to her, but he hadn't taken more than a few steps when there was a sudden rumble from inside the cave and the dragon appeared.

It was actually much smaller than George

had expected – not a lot larger than his horse. It was bright green in colour, with a peculiar, misshapen body. Its wings, for example, were far too small to allow it to fly. On one wing there was a pink ring and on the other a red one. It had two rather squat legs and claws and a long, serpent-like neck. But the only really menacing thing about it was its teeth, which were white and very sharp.*

When the princess saw the dragon, she closed her eyes and waited for the end. But George wasn't afraid. 'Oh dragon!' he exclaimed. 'I see you have dined well over the years. But maybe so many free meals have clouded your judgement. Do you really mean to eat this young girl?'

The dragon growled uncertainly. The girl opened her eyes.

'God did not create people to be served

---

* The most accurate picture of the dragon was painted in the fifteenth century by an Italian named Uccello. If you have any doubts about the accuracy of my description, you can see it for yourself at the National Gallery in London.

up for the pleasure of wild animals,' George continued. 'And as a creature of God, you should be ashamed of yourself. It's only because you were created by Him that I don't take out my sword and cut off your head right now. But even animals should be given a chance to repent.'

Smoke trickled out of the dragon's nostrils and formed a question mark over its head.

'Enough of this foolishness!' George untied the girl and helped her to her feet. Then he took a ribbon from her dress and tied it round the dragon's neck. 'Let us go back to Silene and talk this over.' He bowed to the princess. 'It seems to me, my lady,' he continued, 'that you will make a much wiser and kinder ruler than your father. Your actions have shown that much already.'

There was a tremendous uproar in Silene when George returned. First of all, the people saw the princess walking next to him. Everyone had assumed she was dead. Her

obituary had already appeared in several ce-
lebrity magazines. But even more astonishing was the sight of the dragon itself, wad-
dling timidly behind at the end of a ribbon.
Was this what they had been afraid of for so
many years? How could they have listened
to the king and the councillors who had in
some ways been as bad as the dragon itself,
feeding so easily on their fears?

From that day on, nothing in Silene was the same. Indeed, by the end of the week, the entire town had converted to Christianity.

And so, in fact, had the dragon.

Shortly after that, the king retired from the throne and his daughter became queen. All the ministers and councillors were sacked and, although a couple of them stayed behind to write their autobiographies and a

couple more were invited to join the board of the local bank, the rest of them left town. None of them were missed.

The princess married a local prince and the two of them ruled well and wisely for many years. As for the dragon, it ended its days in the palace gardens, a friend and playmate of the queen's children. It also became a confirmed vegetarian.

THE WASHER AT THE FORD

Celtic

In the hours before a battle, a great peace descends upon the men who may be about to die. Those who live will remember it long afterwards. Of course they are afraid. As the sun sinks in the sky, a certain darkness creeps not just across the hillside, but into their very souls. They see the blades of imaginary swords biting into their flesh. They feel the pain of their limbs being severed, the bone being cut in two, and wonder what it will be like to lie there in the long grass, watching their lifeblood spread all around them. Or perhaps it will be an arrow, striking them down without warning – in the throat, in the chest. How much will it hurt? How long will they suffer before they are released into the comfort of death? They know that many of the men they see around them, friends they have travelled with for years, may never see the sun set again. Here they are, drinking wine, scowling, warming themselves by the fire. They are human. They are alive. Tomorrow they may

be nothing. Even the thoughts they are thinking may become nothing, just blackness, in
a few hours' time.

So it was on the evening before the
Battle of Gabhra. Gabhra today is known
as Garristown in north-west County Dublin,
but this was almost two thousand years
ago, when Ireland was young and strange
creatures, witches and demons still walked
among men. Many of the *fianna* had no idea
why this battle was about to take place. Nor
did they care. They were here and nobody
could stop what was about to happen. That
was all that mattered.

The *fianna* was a warrior band. Some
called them mercenaries – others had names
that were worse than that. True, there were
robbers and bandits who rode with them,
but there were also aristocrats: young noble-
men still waiting to inherit their fathers'
estates. Like the ancient samurai in Japan
or Robin Hood's merry men in medieval
England, they would fight for their country

when they were needed. And they liked to think of themselves as poets. In order to join the *fianna*, you actually had to learn twelve books of poetry off by heart! Wasn't that proof enough?

There were other, more physical tests. A

would-be *fénnid*, as the recruits were called, would have to prove that he could walk over dead branches and leaves without making a sound. He would have to pull a vicious thorn out of his own foot while he was running – without stopping or even slowing down. But the most dangerous ordeal involved a pit dug in the ground. The recruit would climb down so that he stood waist-deep and would be given a shield and a hazel stick. Nine men with spears would surround the pit and, at a given signal, the test would begin. A fight . . . sometimes to the death. The *fénnid* would weave and dive between the spear thrusts. If he was wounded even once, he would be considered to have failed.

In fact, at sunrise the *fianna* would be fighting against the forces of the High King of Ireland, a man called Cairbre Lifechair. The king's daughter had recently got married and it was the custom at the time to pay a tribute to the *fianna* on the day of the wedding. The High King had refused. In return, the *fianna* had killed one of the king's servants. How easily a simple argument had turned into a full-scale war! Lifechair had summoned up his army and both sides had assembled at the damp, foggy swampland around Gabhra. At dawn they would settle their differences once and for all.

The men had eaten their supper. Soon they would sleep. But now they were talking. Whatever they might be thinking, there wasn't a single one of them who wasn't glad to be there. For they were in the company of one of the great heroes of the *fianna*, a man known all over Ireland. His name was Oscar, and although he was still in his twenties there were already epic poems and songs that had been inspired by his exploits. His father was Oisín, another legendary fighter, and he was also there although, unlike his son, Oisín liked to keep himself out of sight.

It was often said that when Oscar was

young, in his early teens, he had been so clumsy and unreliable that none of the older warriors had wanted to ride with him. But by the time he was twenty, all that had changed. He was Oscar the Brave, Oscar the Victorious, Oscar who had never lost in battle or hand-to-hand combat. He still looked younger than his true age, with long fair hair tumbling over his shoulders, a thin, chiselled face and very bright blue eyes. He was famous for his laughter and his carefree attitude to the dangers that lay ahead.

And yet tonight he was unusually quiet. It was as if he was lost in thought, and when someone proposed a song, Oscar shook his head slowly and crept away to sit in the darkness. Some of the men were disturbed by this, but another warrior, a man called Dáire, scowled at them. 'He's just preserving his strength for tomorrow. And if you had any sense, you'd do the same. We need to sleep. Unless you want to fall asleep, perhaps permanently, on the field.'

But secretly Dáire
was concerned. From the
moment Oscar had arrived that
day, he hadn't been quite himself. Dáire was
ten years older than his friend, dark and

battle-scarred. He liked to think of himself as Oscar's older brother. The two of them had been through many adventures together. He knew when something was wrong.

So, when he was sure nobody was looking, he went over to Oscar and sat down beside him. For a while, neither of them spoke. Dáire took out a wineskin and drank. He offered it to his friend. Once again, Oscar shook his head.

'What's the matter?' Dáire asked.

There was no answer. Dáire was about to ask the question a second time when Oscar spoke. He was gazing straight ahead of him as if trying to find something in the darkness of the night. 'I was thinking of some of the monsters I have encountered in my life,' he said. His voice was soft. He had the ability to sing even when he was talking. It was a great talent. Dáire had often listened in wonderment as Oscar recited his father's verse. 'I was just wondering which of them was the worst.'

'Do you mean the ugliest or the most dangerous?'

'I don't know what I mean.'

'Then why are you even thinking such things? There'll be time enough for monsters after the battle is done. Now – Cairbre Lifechair . . . there's a monster for you. Calls himself a king, but puts us to all this bother and throws away the life of his men just because he's too mean to pay for a wedding!'

'I will tell you what happened to me today, Dáire. But only you. Promise me you won't speak to anyone else.'

'What are you talking about, Oscar?' Dáire raised the skin to his lips and drank heavily. Whatever happened tomorrow, he wasn't going to leave behind any of his wine.

'I'm talking about the washer at the ford,' Oscar said.

He paused. And then he began his tale.

'As I was riding here, I had to cross a ford. I'd been following the river for some distance and the water was deep and fast-flowing. It

was the only way
to the other side. Well,
there was a woman sitting there. She was
washing some clothes.'

'An old hag, I'll bet—'

'No. She was young and quite pretty. She
had fair hair like mine, only lighter. And her
skin was very white. I assumed she must be
married, because she was washing a man's
clothing.'

'Her husband's?'

'That's what I thought.' Oscar took a deep

breath. 'Anyway, my horse
needed water, so I dismounted
and sat with her a while. The sun
was shining and I was in no great
hurry. I knew that I was only a few
miles from here. For a time, neither of
us spoke. The woman continued washing
her clothes and I sat beside her.

'But then she turned to me. "You're on
your way to battle!" she said.

'I nodded. I imagined that she must have seen many soldiers going past. It would have been obvious that a battle was about to take place.

'"Are you afraid?" she asked.

'"I'm not afraid of anything," I replied.

'"Is that so?"

'She was mocking me. I could hear it in her voice. And maybe that made me forget myself. "I have never yet come across a beast or a monster that could frighten me," I told her.

'"Oh yes? And what is the worst monster you have ever met?" she asked.'

Oscar came to a halt. Dáire had listened to all this in silence. He could see that his friend was still deep in thought, so he tried to make light of it all. 'You should have grabbed hold of the wench and pushed her into the ford, along with all her washing,' he said. 'That would have put an end to her insolence.'

'Perhaps. But there was something about her question that made me think. I have come across many monsters in my life and I have vanquished them all, starting with the ugly giant with the deerskins.'

'His head rolled down the hill!' Dáire had often heard Oscar describe the incident, particularly when the two of them were drunk. It never failed to make them laugh.

More than eight feet tall, the giant had been travelling up a hill in Western Ireland, carrying two piles of deerskins under his arms. The giant had a truly hideous face, with fat, deformed lips, swollen eyes and a nose that seemed to have been used as a punchbag.

His skin was mottled and his hair, a nasty ginger colour, hung over his forehead like a mop. His shirt was stretched tight over his massive belly and his jacket hung loose as if it had been torn apart. The giant was going up the hill. Oscar was coming down. The path was narrow and there was mud on both sides. Inevitably, there had been an argument. Although Oscar was tiny in comparison with the giant – for he was only fifteen when this had happened – he had refused to step out of the way.

'You step aside, Mr Giant, unless you want to feel the edge of my sword.'

'You step aside, rude boy, unless you want to encounter my club.' And dropping the deerskins, the giant had produced a club so huge it could have been cut from the trunk of a tree.

'I'm warning you, giant—'

'Be silent, boy . . .'

The fight had been a brief one. The giant had swung his club. Oscar had ducked, then leaped up, swinging his sword. The slope of the hill had given him extra height, and the blade had found its target in the giant's neck, severing his head. There was an ex plosion, a fountain of blood. The giant's head had come clean off and, as Dáire had rightly said, it had rolled all the way down the hill and into a nearby convent, where the nuns had been about to have lunch. They were still in hysterics an hour later.

'Was that the worst monster?' Dáire asked. All around him the *fianna* were curling up for the night, covering themselves with their heavy cloaks. A few fires were still flickering and there were lights also, far away on the other side of the swamp, a reminder of the men, very similar to them, waiting for what the next day might bring.

'It might have been,' Oscar said. 'But then again I could have chosen the wild boar at Ben Bulben.'

'Another fine candidate.' Dáire nodded.

This was another famous story. Oscar had been in the forests near Sligo, hunting with his grandfather, the great hero Fionn mac Cumhaill,* and some of the other *fianna*. Suddenly a huge boar came crashing out of the undergrowth. It was a dreadful creature, covered in iron-grey hair, with burning eyes, a wet, upturned snout, and tusks that curved out of its head like poisoned swords. Before anyone could do anything, it had charged at one of Fionn's oldest friends – a man called Diarmaid – and slammed both tusks into his stomach. Diarmaid screamed in agony and fell to his knees, blood gushing into his lap. The animal seemed to screech in triumph, wheeling round and looking for the next person to attack.

One of the younger hunters threw a spear at the beast, but it simply snapped in half, bouncing off the boar's back. The creature was incredibly fast. It charged a second

---

* Pronounced Finn McCool

time and suddenly the young man was on the ground, crying out, with a broken leg. A third man threw himself at the boar, pulling out a knife. The boar wheeled round, throwing him off, then prepared to charge him too.

There might have been more deaths and injuries that day if it hadn't been for Oscar. He had whipped out his own knife and charged forward, placing himself between the animal and its intended victim. The boar had no choice. Letting out another high-pitched squeal, it lowered its head and charged at Oscar, the pointed tusks aiming straight for him.

To everyone, including his grandfather, it looked as if Oscar was about to be cut in half. But at the last moment, he dived flat to the ground, disappearing between the boar's legs. An instant later he twisted round so that he was now underneath the monster, with its soft underbelly above him.

As quick as lightning, he lashed out. His knife slit the boar from neck to groin. The boar howled as all the insides fell out of it, covering Oscar with a tangled knot of steaming, bloody intestines.

The beast took one final step and died.

Diarmaid didn't survive that day. But it was also the day that Oscar was confirmed as Fionn's worthy grandson and a hero in his own right.

'You told the washer about the boar?' Dáire asked. It was growing late and he wondered where all this was going.

'I told her about the boar,' Oscar replied. 'I told her about the giant. And for good measure I told her about some of the other kings and warriors I have fought against and about Cairbre Lifechair. I de-scribed the howling pack of man-eating wolves that once stalked me through the eternal forest near Lough Dreary, and the three-headed creature, the *ellen*, that came out of the Cave of Cruachan.

'But the washer at the ford just laughed at me. Nothing I said to her seemed to make any impression. And finally, she looked up at me and she said, "There are worse monsters than all of these," and even as she spoke the words, I noticed something. The clothes she was washing . . . Her hands were covered in blood.'

'What?' Dáire had been nodding off to sleep, lulled by the wine. But when he heard what Oscar had just said, he sat bolt upright and there was something in his face that none of the *fianna* would have seen for many a long day.

He was afraid.

'She was washing blood out of the clothes,' Oscar said quietly. 'And suddenly I understood. I suppose I should have seen it all along. Even so, I couldn't stop myself asking, "Whose clothes are those?"

'The woman looked straight at me and it was then that I saw it. She was not beautiful. She was cold and empty. Her eyes were as black and as unforgiving as a bottomless pool in the heart of winter. Her smile was the smile of a death's head. "The clothes are yours, Oscar," she said. And with that she was gone. She simply crumpled in front of

me. The wind carried her away.'

There was a long silence. The hillside around Oscar and Dáire was now strewn with sleeping figures. But they knew that neither of them would find any rest that night.

'She was a banshee,' Oscar said, and fell silent.

Banshees were known to every child in the land. Meet a banshee and you would be dead within twenty-four hours. There could be no argument and no escape. A banshee was the herald of your death.

And so it was to be. The Battle of Gabhra began the next morning and very soon Oscar found himself in hand-to-hand combat with Cairbre Lifechair. He fought bravely and even managed to wound the king so badly that he would later die of his wounds. But he was also careless. For just a moment he lowered his guard and the king, though crippled and bleeding, thrust his spear through Oscar's heart, killing him instantly. The day went badly for the rest of the *fianna* too.

They lost the battle and that was the end of their power in the country of Ireland.

Somehow Dáire survived. He made his way back to his home in County Kildare and spent the rest of his days a farmer. But he never forgot that last night and the story that his old friend had told him. The washer at the ford had asked Oscar to name the greatest monster. He hadn't realized that he was talking to it all the time.

THE GORGON'S HEAD

Greek

There was once a king called Polydectes who ruled over a small but very attractive island called Seriphos. In fact, it must be said, one of the least attractive things on the island was the king himself. Like many rulers in Ancient Greece, he was cruel and thoughtless and took what he wanted without considering anyone else.

And one of the things that he wanted was a woman who happened to live in his palace. Her name was Danaë, and as well as being very beautiful she was also very vulnerable as she was a foreigner who had come here quite by chance while he, of course, was the king. Danaë was in fact the victim of a shipwreck. She has been washed up on the island a few years before with no money and no one to support her apart from a young son, Perseus. The king had given Danaë a room in the palace and had forced Perseus to become a soldier in his army. That way he had them both where he wanted them.

For Polydectes had fallen in love with

Danaë and was determined to make her his wife. Unfortunately, Danaë didn't quite have the same feelings about Polydectes. This was hardly surprising. The king was overweight. He had a foul temper. But worst of all, he had very bad breath. It was said that his breath could stop a Cyclops at ten paces – and don't forget that for a Cyclops ten paces is a very long way indeed.

Left to himself, Polydectes would have forced Danaë to marry him, but of course there was Perseus to consider. The boy was strong, afraid of nothing and very quick-tempered . . . in short, just the sort to let fly with a sword if anyone laid a finger on his mother. Worse still, he was very popular on the island, and there would have been an uproar if something horrible had 'accidentally' happened to him.

The king thought about it for a time and at last he came up with a plan. He announced his marriage, but pretended that he was going to marry the daughter of a friend of his.

He then threw a great banquet and invited everyone in the neighbourhood.

Of course, everybody brought gifts. And of course, the gifts (like so many wedding presents) were completely useless. He got no fewer than fifteen goblets and seven wine jugs, for example, and he already had more goblets and wine jugs than he knew what to do with.

Nonetheless, there was no mistaking the value of the presents, which were all made of gold or silver or onyx or the finest marble. Everyone had done their best to show how loyal they were to the king and how much they valued his friendship. Everyone, that is, with one exception.

Poor Perseus couldn't possibly have afforded anything made of gold or silver, even if it had been very small. The soldier's salary that he received barely paid for a pot of sword polish – and he was expected to keep his weapons bright and shiny whenever he went on parade. It was as much as he could

do to dress up smartly for the occasion. Even a new robe and a decent pair of sandals took a great chunk out of his savings. Of course, Polydectes knew this. It was all part of his plan.

'What, no wedding present?' he shouted, when Perseus presented himself at the wedding feast.

There were gasps of surprise around the banqueting tables.

'I'm very sorry, Your Majesty . . .' Perseus began.

'Don't you know that it is a tradition to bring your sovereign a present when he decides to get married?'

'I'm afraid I don't have any money.'

'That's no excuse. You could have borrowed money. You could have stolen money . . . from one of our enemies, of course. Coming here empty handed is an outrage. It's nothing short of treason!'

'I really didn't mean to insult you, sire. And you can have anything you want for your wedding present. You only have to name it.'

'Anything?' Polydectes asked, raising an eyebrow.

'Anything,' Perseus said.

'Anything?' Polydectes insisted, raising the other eyebrow.

'Anything in the world,' said Perseus.

This was exactly what the king had planned. He knew that putting Perseus on the spot in front of the other guests would fluster him and that he would make a promise he couldn't keep. In other words, he had designed a noose and young Perseus had put his head right into it.

'All right,' he exclaimed, 'Then what I would like for my wedding present is the Gorgon's head. If you want to prove your loyalty to me, bring me the head of the Gorgon.'

There was a stunned silence in the room. The wedding guests, stretched out at the tables (which was the way in Ancient Greek banquets), gasped. Nobody moved.

'Very well, Your Majesty,' Perseus said. 'If the head of the Gorgon is what you want, the head of the Gorgon is what you shall have.'

And with that, Perseus turned on his heel and stormed out of the room. The king waited until he was sure he had gone, then grabbed hold of his mother. 'I want you to come to my wedding,' he announced.

'It's my pleasure, Your Majesty,' Danaë muttered.

'Of course it's your pleasure, darling. You're the one I'm marrying!'

The Three Gorgons

Of all the beasts, giants, dragons and demi-gods in Ancient Greece, the Gorgons were perhaps the most terrifying. They petrified people – quite literally.

There were three Gorgons. Stheno and Euryate and Medusa. The first two were immortal, meaning they would live forever. The third and most fearsome, Medusa, was not. She was the only one that Perseus had any chance of being able to kill.

Strangely, the Gorgons had once been three very attractive young girls.

Medusa, in particular, had been quite lovely, with fair hair, blue eyes and a gorgeous smile. Unfortunately, she had chosen to fall in love with Poseidon, the god of the sea, and as if this wasn't bad enough (mortals were always unwise to get too close to the gods) she had slept with him in the temple of Athene, the Goddess of Wisdom. This had been hugely unwise. To punish her for behaving improperly in her temple, Athene had turned her – and her sisters with her – into the Gorgons. Gone were the white dresses, the daisies and the ponytails. A single wave of the hand and they were monsters.

Hideous monsters. Instead of teeth they had sharp tusks like wild boars. Their hands

were made of bronze and golden wings sprouted from their shoulders. But what was most remarkable about the horrors that they had become was their hair. It was made of living snakes, slimy green and silver, with hissing tongues and gleaming eyes. There were dozens of them, sprouting out of the Gorgons' skulls, writhing over their foreheads, curling round their necks and twisting over their shoulders.

If anyone ever had the misfortune to set eyes on a Gorgon . . . they did nothing. For this was the cruellest part of the trick that King Polydectes had played on Perseus. Everyone who saw the face of the Gorgon became so frightened that they instantly turned to stone, and he knew that Perseus would never get anywhere near them. Just one glance in their direction and he would be doomed.

The Goddess of Wisdom

Perseus had no idea that he had been tricked. Nor did he know what was happening to his poor mother while he was away. And he had been away for a long time. He had travelled far and searched for a long time but he had found no trace of either Medusa or her ugly sisters. Nobody seemed to know where they lived. Most of the travellers he had encountered seemed unwilling to talk about them at all.

One night he found himself sitting under a tree on the edge of a swamp in an unknown country. He had no money with him and so he was unable to stay in an inn or a hotel – even if he had stumbled on such a thing. His only food, as usual, was the fruit and the berries that he found along the way. He was cold and he was alone. For the first time he was beginning to wonder if he hadn't been a bit hasty in agreeing to the king's request.

It was at that moment that a figure

suddenly appeared, stepping out of the flames of the meagre bonfire he had built to keep himself warm. It was a woman, tall and imperious, with bright, purposeful eyes. Her head was covered by a silver helmet and she was carrying a spear and a gleaming shield. Perseus recognized her at once. Like every child, he had been taught about the gods and goddesses, although he had never expected to meet one. This woman had to be Athene. She was the Goddess of Wisdom.

'Perseus,' she said, standing in front of him, 'I've come to help you. You have a good heart and I know that one day you will be a great hero, but you are also young and foolish and you have allowed King Polydectes to trick you.'

'Thank you, great Athene,' Perseus said. 'I do need your help. You see, I'm looking for—'

'I know who you're looking for,' Athene interrupted. 'I am, after all, the Goddess of Wisdom. And it's lucky you didn't interrupt my father so rudely. He would have turned you into an acorn or a frog or something. But as I say, I've decided to help you and I'll begin by saying that the only way to find the Gorgons is to ask their sisters – the Grey Ones.'

'Where will I find them?' Perseus asked.

'By a happy coincidence, they live in the swamp, a few minutes from here. But listen to me, Perseus. You have to be very careful how you kill Medusa. Because anyone who sees her turns to stone.'

'You mean . . . I can't even look at her?'

'Not directly. No.' Athene laughed briefly and without much humour. 'Polydectes didn't tell you that, did he! But it doesn't matter. I can show you what to do.'

'It's very kind of you, mighty Athene,' Perseus said.

'Don't mention it. As a matter of fact, I've never cared much for Medusa and it's about time someone did away with her. Now listen to what I have to tell you, Perseus. Your life will depend on it . . .'

LEGENDS

The Grey Ones

A short while later, Perseus crept up on the Grey Ones, who were sitting beside a bog arguing. They were always arguing. The Grey Ones weren't exactly monsters but they were certainly very strange. They had been born with grey hair (which is how they got their name) and they had only one eye and one tooth between the three of them. They were called Enyo, Pemphredo and Deino.

As Perseus approached, this is what he heard.

'Can I have the tooth, please, Enyo?' Pemphredo was saying.

'Why?' Enyo asked.

'Because I want to eat an apple.'

'But I'm eating a toffee.'

'You can suck the toffee. I want the tooth!'

'All right. All right. Here it is, then.'

'I can't see it.'

'Haven't you got the eye?'

'I've got the eye,' Deino
said.

'Let me have it,' Pemphredo demanded.

'No. I'm looking at something.'

The argument continued endlessly and
Perseus guessed that the three old hags
must have had the same conversation every
day of their lives. Making no sound, he
tiptoed up behind them and snatched away
both the eye and the tooth.

'Who is it?' Enyo demanded.

'Bite him!' Pemphredo exclaimed.

'I can't!' Deino cried. 'He's got the tooth!'

'All right,' Perseus said. 'I've got your eye and your tooth and I won't let you have them back until you tell me where I can find your sister, the Gorgon Medusa.'

The three Grey Ones got up and tried to grab him, but being unable to see they only grabbed each other. Eventually they sat down again, banging their fists in the mud and wailing with frustration.

'If you don't tell me what I want to know,' Perseus continued, 'I'll throw your eye and your tooth away and you'll never see or bite anyone again.'

'All right!'

'All right!'

'All right!'

The Grey Ones tried to grind their teeth. But since that was impossible, they ground their gums instead.

'Go to the Land of the Hyperboreans,' Enyo said. Her voice was shrill and bitter. 'There's a big cave in a valley there.

You can't miss it.'

'That's where you'll find her,' Pemphredo added. 'Just make sure you get a good look at her.'

'Look her straight in the eyes!' Deino giggled. 'You'll never forget your first sight of Medusa.'

Perseus gave them back their eye and their tooth and left them, their laughter echoing in his ears. The Grey Ones were still cackling to themselves, thinking how clever they had been, when he arrived in the Land of the Hyperboreans.

Medusa

Athene had not only told Perseus how to destroy the Gorgon, she had given him the means. As he approached Medusa's cave, trying not to make any sound, he was carrying the goddess's brightly polished shield in one hand and his own army sword in the other.

He knew that this must be where Medusa lived. He was in a gulley, a narrow cleft in the rocky landscape that was filled with stone people, some trapped as they turned to run, others frozen in horror, their mouths open, the screams still on their lips. It was as if they had been photographed in the last second of their life. Their reaction in that second had been caught for eternity. One young soldier had covered his face, but then he had tried to peep through his fingers. His stone hand still shuttered his stone eyes. A farmer with a scythe stood rigid with a puzzled smile, his stone fingers curled around the weapon, still trying to swing it through the air. There were stone women and stone children. It was like a crazy open-air museum.

Perseus saw the mouth of a large cave yawning darkly at him. Holding the shield more tightly than ever, he climbed up the gentle slope and, taking a deep breath, entered the gloom.

'Medusa!' he called out. His voice sounded lost in the shadows.

Something moved at the back of the cave.

'Medusa!' he repeated.

Now he could hear breathing and the sound of hissing.

'I am Perseus!' he announced.

'Perseus!' came a deep, throaty voice from the back of the cave. It was followed by a soft giggling. 'Have you come to see me?'

The Gorgon stepped forward into the light. For a dreadful moment, Perseus was tempted to look up at her, to meet her eyes. But with all his strength he kept his head turned away as Athene had instructed him and instead concentrated on the reflection in the shield. He could see her green skin, her poisonous red eyes and her yellow teeth, all reflected in the polished bronze. He lifted the sword.

'Look at me! Look at me!' the Gorgon cried.

Still he kept his eyes on the shield. He took another step into the cave. The reflection was huge, the teeth snarling at him out of the shield. The snakes writhed furiously, hissing with the sound of red-hot needles being plunged into water.

'Look at me! Look at me!'

How could he find her when all he could see was the reflection? Surely it would be easier to kill her if he took one quick look at her, just to make sure that he didn't miss . . .

'Yes. That's right. I'm here!'

'No!'

With a despairing cry, Perseus swung wildly with his sword. He felt the sharp steel bite into flesh and bone. The Gorgon screamed. The snakes exploded around her head as the whole thing flew from her shoulders, bounced against the cave wall and rolled to the ground. A fountain of blood spouted out of her neck as her body crumpled. Then at last it was over. With his eyes still fixed

on the shield, Perseus picked up the grim trophy of his victory and dropped it into a heavy sack.

The Gorgon's Head

Perseus had spent months looking for the Gorgon and he had many other adventures on his way back to Seriphos. And so a whole year had passed by the time he returned.

The first person he saw on the island was an old fisherman who was just bringing in the morning catch. His name was Dictys and by coincidence it had been he who had first discovered Perseus and his mother when they were washed ashore. The two greeted each other like old friends.

'My dear Dictys,' Perseus said. 'Here I am, back at last. Now tell me, has the king married?'

'No,' the fisherman said. 'King Polydectes lives alone.'

'And how is my mother?' Perseus asked.

At this, the old man burst into tears. 'Oh Master Perseus!' he cried. 'It was your mother that the wicked king wished to marry. Once you were gone, he tried to force her into his bed, and when she refused he turned her into a slave. For a whole year now she's been worked to the bone in the palace kitchens, carrying and cleaning. It's a terrible thing, Master Perseus. The king just laughs at her . . .'

'He does, does he?' Perseus said through gritted teeth. 'We'll soon see about that!'

Throwing the bundle that he carried over his shoulder, Perseus strode into the palace and straight into the great hall where King Polydectes was sitting on his throne.

'Greetings, Your Majesty!' he called out to the astonished monarch. 'It is I, Perseus, returned after twelve long months. I bring with me the present that you asked for.'

'The Gorgon's head?' Polydectes muttered. 'A likely story!'

'Don't you believe me, sire?' Perseus asked.

'Certainly not,' the king said.

'Would you believe your own eyes?'

'Have you got it there?' The king pointed at the sack.

'See for yourself.'

And with that, Perseus lifted the Gorgon's head out of the sack and held it up for the king to see.

'It's . . .' King Polydectes got no further than that. What was he about to say? It's hideous? It's not possible? Nobody would ever know. The next moment there was a stone statue leaning out of the throne, a stone sneer on its stone face and one stone eyebrow raised in disbelief.

Perseus wondered what would happen next. He had, after all, just assassinated the king. He was completely surrounded by the courtiers and the royal guard and he was prepared to turn the Gorgon's head on anyone who tried to arrest him. But no sooner had Polydectes been frozen than there was a great cheering that began around the throne

and spread through-out the palace. For it turned out that everyone on the island was tired of their cruel and scheming monarch. Perseus had finally got rid of him and, by popular acclaim, he was invited to become the new king.

But Perseus had had enough of Seriphos. Instead he chose Dictys to inherit the throne on the grounds that an honest fisherman would be just the man to rule over a kingdom – and certainly one that was entirely surrounded by water. He was reunited with his mother and, laden with gifts and various pieces of royal treasure, the two of them set off for new adventures. Eventually, he became the King of Mycenae, for Athene had been right. He had a good heart and had been born to be a hero.

He gave the Gorgon's head to the goddess and she magically turned it into part of her armour and wore it to terrify her enemies in battle. Dictys ruled Seriphos long and well.

As for Polydectes, he was put in the palace garden as a pleasing ornament, and he is probably still there to this day.

TEN BRILLIANT BEASTS AND MARVELLOUS MONSTERS

YOU MIGHT NOT HAVE HEARD OF

. . . but I'm afraid I've made one of them up. Can you spot the intruder?

AL-MI'RAJ

A mythical beast found in Islamic poetry, the Al-mi'raj is a large yellow rabbit with a single horn, like that of a unicorn. It may look harmless, but the Al-mi'raj is extremely aggressive and can kill and eat animals far larger than itself.

BONNACON

This mythical animal from Asia is similar in appearance to a bison, but with long, curly horns. Its most unusual feature is its dung, which is constantly on fire.

BARBEGAZI

A variety of gnome found in Swiss folklore. They have extremely large feet, which are useful for skiing through the mountains, or surfing down avalanches.

CHARYBDIS

A sea monster from Greek mythology, which is basically a giant mouth that swallows large amounts of water (and any unsuspecting ships that might be floating in it) and then spits it out as whirlpools.

THE CHONCHON

An interesting creature from Mapuche Indian mythology, the Chonchon is a disembodied human head. It uses its extremely large ears as wings.

PUCKWUDGIE

A small troll-like demon of Native American origin, the Puckwudgie has smooth, grey skin that has been known to glow in the dark. It can create fire and change its shape and is known for causing trouble!

ROMPO

In some African and Indian folklore Rompo has human ears, the head of a rabbit, a skeletal body, the arms of a badger and the legs of a bear. It is said to feed on human flesh and sing as it eats.

NONTHYA

A High Priestess in Nubian mythology, this old hag had three eyes. One could see the past, one could see the future and one was blind. She lived in a cave with a talking snake.

AMMIT

Meaning 'devourer' or 'bone eater', Ammit is an Egyptian demon who is part lion, part hippo and part crocodile. In Egyptian mythology, when a person died their heart was weighed by Anubis on a pair of scales. If the heart was lighter than a feather, the person could continue to the afterlife – if not, they were eaten by Ammit.

TYPHON

The most deadly monster of Greek

mythology, Typhon is as tall as the stars, with the heads of one hundred dragons extending from each hand. His lower half is made of enormous vipers and his whole body covered with wings.

LEGENDS

BATTLES AND QUESTS

Brother fighting brother. Man slaying beast.
Tales of epic **quests** and furious **battles**
have been told throughout time –
Theseus and the **Minotaur**; **King Arthur**
and the **Black Knight**; Romulus and Remus,
and the **screams** of the Great Bell of Peking.
But there are some evils that no sword
can defeat . . .

Another action-packed retelling from Anthony Horowitz